Karen's Black Cat

**Other books by
Ann M. Martin**

P. S. Longer Letter Later
(written with Paula Danziger)
Leo the Magnificat
Rachel Parker, Kindergarten Show-off
Eleven Kids, One Summer
Ma and Pa Dracula
Yours Turly, Shirley
Ten Kids, No Pets
With You and Without You
Me and Katie (the Pest)
Stage Fright
Inside Out
Bummer Summer

For older readers:

Missing Since Monday
Just a Summer Romance
Slam Book

THE BABY-SITTERS CLUB series
THE BABY-SITTERS CLUB mysteries
THE KIDS IN MS. COLMAN'S CLASS series
BABY-SITTERS LITTLE SISTER series
(see inside book covers for a complete listing)

Little Sister

Karen's Black Cat
Ann M. Martin

Illustrations by Susan Crocca Tang

A
LITTLE APPLE
PAPERBACK

SCHOLASTIC INC.
New York Toronto London Auckland Sydney

ISBN 0-590-50054-6

12 11 10 9 8 7 6 5 4 3 2 1   8 9/9 0 1 2 3/0

Printed in the U.S.A.   40
First Scholastic printing, October 1998

*The author gratefully acknowledges
Stephanie Calmenson
for her help
with this book.*

Karen's Black Cat

A Visit to the Vet

It was a Saturday morning in October. I was sitting alone in the waiting room of Dr. Smith's office. Well, I was not really alone. Some people with their pets were there too. Dr. Smith is a veterinarian.

I saw three dogs: a Scottie, a Westie, and a Dalmatian.

I saw a green-and-yellow parakeet who kept saying, "Hello! Hello!"

And I saw a brown rabbit who wiggled his nose a lot.

Elizabeth, my stepmother, was in the examining room with our cat, Boo-Boo. Boo-Boo is an old gray tiger cat. He can be crabby sometimes. That is why I did not go into the office.

"We find that nervous animals do better with fewer people around," Dr. Smith told us when we came in.

So I was sitting in the waiting room, thinking. Here are some things you might like to know about me. I am seven years old. I have blonde hair, blue eyes, and freckles. Also, I am a glasses-wearer. Hmm. I wonder if Boo-Boo needs glasses.

Before I got glasses, I had headaches that made me cranky. Boo-Boo has been crankier than usual lately. And he has been eating more and sleeping less. Maybe his eyes are his problem. I tried to picture Boo-Boo wearing my glasses. First I pictured him in my blue glasses. They are the ones I wear for reading. Then I pictured him in my pink glasses. They are the ones I wear the rest of the time. I decided the color did not mat-

ter. Boo-Boo in glasses was a silly sight!

A cold wet nose poked my hand. It was the Dalmatian. His tail was wagging.

"I hope you do not mind. He is very friendly," said his owner.

"I don't mind. What is his name?" I asked.

"Spot. I know it is not very original, but it fits," said his owner.

I reached down to pet Spot. I was glad that I would not be able to introduce him to Boo-Boo. Boo-Boo might hiss or show his claws. It is no fun having a crabby pet.

Just then Elizabeth came out of the examining room. Boo-Boo was in his carrier. When they passed the other animals he did not even hiss. That was not like him.

"Good-bye, everyone!" I said. I held the door open for Elizabeth. Then I asked, "Will Boo-Boo be okay?"

"Dr. Smith is worried about him," replied Elizabeth. "She has run some tests and will call us with the results later this week."

I felt worried about Boo-Boo. I knew the rest of my family was worried too. That is a lot of people. Boo-Boo and I are part of a big family of people and pets. I will tell you who they are.

Boo-Boo's Family

Guess what. Boo-Boo has one family, but I have two. Here's why.

A long time ago when I was little, my family was Mommy, Daddy, Andrew, and me. (Andrew is my little brother. He is four going on five.) We all lived together in a big house in Stoneybrook, Connecticut.

Then Mommy and Daddy got divorced. Mommy moved with Andrew and me to a little house not far away. She met a very nice man named Seth. She and Seth got married, and now Seth is my stepfather.

At first, the four of us lived in the little house with all our pets. The pets are Emily Junior, who is my pet rat; Bob, who is Andrew's hermit crab; Midgie, who is Seth's dog; and Rocky, who is Seth's cat. (Rocky is a lot friendlier than Boo-Boo.)

Things changed last spring when Seth took a very good job for a few months in Chicago. We all went there together. But I missed Stoneybrook too much, so I came back.

I was lucky that I had somewhere to go. You see, I have another house and another family. Now I am living in the big house. Daddy stayed here after he and Mommy got divorced. (It is the house he grew up in.) Then he met and married Elizabeth, which is how she became my stepmother.

Elizabeth was married once before and has four children. They are my stepbrothers and stepsister: David Michael, who is seven, like me; Kristy, who is thirteen and the best stepsister ever; and Sam and Charlie, who are so old they are in high school.

I also have a little sister, Emily Michelle,

who is two and a half. I love her a lot, which is why I named my rat after her. Daddy and Elizabeth adopted her from a faraway country called Vietnam.

The other person living at the big house is Nannie. She is Elizabeth's mother, which makes her my stepgrandmother. She came to live at the big house to help with Emily. But now she helps everyone with everything.

Of course you know about Boo-Boo already. But there are other pets at the big house. They are Shannon, David Michael's big Bernese mountain dog puppy; Scout, our training-to-be-a-guide-dog puppy; Crystal Light the Second, my goldfish; and Goldfishie, Andrew's porcupine. (Just kidding!) Goldfishie is Andrew's fish, who decided to stay in Stoneybrook too.

Before Andrew went to Chicago, the two of us switched houses almost every month. We spent one month at the big house, then one month at the little house. That is when I gave us our special names. I call us Andrew Two-Two and Karen Two-Two. (I thought

8

up those names after my teacher read a book to our class. It was called *Jacob Two-Two Meets the Hooded Fang*.) I call us those names because we each have two of so many things. We each have two houses and two families with two mommies and two daddies. We have two sets of toys and clothes and books. We have two bicycles, one at each house.

I also have two best friends. Hannie Papadakis lives across the street and one house over from the big house. Nancy Dawes lives next door to the little house. (Hannie and Nancy and I are in the same second-grade class at Stoneybrook Academy. And we play together all the time. That is why we call ourselves the Three Musketeers.)

I am happy with my two families. I wonder if Boo-Boo is happy with his one family. I think he is. After all, he is not *always* cranky. Right now, he is curled up napping in the sun. He looks very peaceful. Boo-Boo, I hope you are okay.

An Excellent Idea

We were eating dinner on Tuesday when the phone rang. Elizabeth answered it. She said hello, and then we heard her say, "Thank you for calling, Dr. Smith."

We stopped talking and listened. But we could not tell what was going on. One moment Elizabeth sounded relieved.

"That is good news," she said into the phone.

The next moment she sounded worried.

"And you are sure there is nothing we can do?"

10

As soon as she hung up, I asked, "What did Dr. Smith say about Boo-Boo?"

"The good news is that Boo-Boo's tests all came back fine. He does not have any sickness she can name," replied Elizabeth.

"Then what is wrong with him?" asked David Michael.

"The sad news is that Boo-Boo is suffering from old age. There is nothing we can do right now to make him feel better. Dr. Smith said we just have to be as kind to him as possible," said Elizabeth.

"Hug Boo-Boo!" suggested Emily.

"I do not think so. Boo-Boo is hiding," I said.

I had not seen Boo-Boo since we sat down to eat. That was probably a good thing. Boo-Boo does not like hugs very much.

"We should respect his need to be by himself," said Daddy.

"Poor old Boo-Boo," said Kristy. "It makes me sad that he does not feel well."

My whole family looked sad.

"I have an idea that could lift our spirits

and maybe Boo-Boo's too," said Elizabeth.

"What is it?" asked Daddy.

"I suggest we think about getting another pet. A kitten might be a good idea," Elizabeth replied.

"That is an excellent idea!" I said.

My spirits were lifted right away.

"I am not so sure," said Daddy. "A new pet in the house could upset Boo-Boo."

"We have had lots of new pets come into the house," said Elizabeth. "Boo-Boo has not been especially friendly, but he did not seem upset."

"That is true. But he is older now," said Daddy.

"I have heard stories about kittens cheering up old cats," said Nannie.

"If Boo-Boo does not like the kitten, he can just ignore it," said Charlie.

"We should take a family vote," said Daddy. "All in favor of getting a kitten, say 'Aye.' "

"Aye!" I said.

So did Elizabeth, Kristy, David Michael,

Sam, Charlie, and Nannie. Emily called out, "Me!"

"The 'ayes' and the 'me' have it," said Daddy. "We can start thinking about looking for a kitten."

"The *Stoneybrook Express* will be out tomorrow," said Sam. "Sometimes there are ads for kittens in it."

The *Stoneybrook Express* is a new community newspaper. I used to deliver the paper with Kristy. But it was too hard for me to have an important job like that and go to school at the same time. So Sam took over.

My family was going to get a kitten. This was very exciting news.

The Purr-fect Kitten

It was my turn to help Nannie clear the table after dinner. I was so excited thinking about our kitten that I almost dropped a plate.

"Good catch!" said Nannie when I caught it.

"Nannie, remember the kittens that were born in the toolshed? I wish we had them now," I said. "I would keep Rosie. She was the bounciest, happiest one."

"I remember how much you liked Rosie,"

replied Nannie. She was at the sink now, rinsing dishes.

Nannie handed me a plate to put in the dishwasher.

"I liked all the kittens — Rosie, Pokey, Tippy, Ruby, and Bob," I said.

"The mother cat was named Growly, wasn't she?" asked Nannie.

She handed me a glass for the dishwasher.

"Yup," I replied. I had forgotten all about the mother cat. "I named her Growly because she growled to protect her kittens. But she was really a nice cat."

I thought about the cats I knew. They were all friendly. Except for Boo-Boo.

"I want to get a nice cat. Not a grumpy one like Boo-Boo," I said.

"We do not know what happened to Boo-Boo before we got him. I doubt he was born cranky. Something may have happened to make him that way," said Nannie.

"We will be very nice to our new cat so she will be friendly when she grows up," I said. "The new cat will play with me. She

16

will be a pretty cat. And she will not be fat like Boo-Boo."

Nannie stopped what she was doing and looked at me.

"Karen, even if Boo-Boo is cranky sometimes and even if he is fat, he is part of our family," she said. "And now he is old. So more than ever he needs all the love we can give him."

"I know," I said. "I just want to love a better cat."

Nannie gave me a Look. I was already sorry I said that. It was not nice. It is just that Boo-Boo is not a fun pet. I wanted my new kitten to be friendly and pretty and funny and everything good a cat could be. I wanted the best, most purr-fect kitten in the whole world!

Meow! Tweet! Boo!

At school on Wednesday, my teacher, Ms. Colman, picked me to take attendance. I love Ms. Colman. She is a gigundoly wonderful teacher. She almost never raises her voice or gets angry at me. Even when I call out in class, she just asks me to use my indoor voice, please. She makes everything interesting. And she asks me to do important jobs such as take attendance.

Ms. Colman handed me the attendance book and a blue pencil. I started checking off names.

I checked off my own name first. Then I checked off Nancy and Hannie. They waved to me from the back of the room. (I used to sit in the back with them. Then I got glasses and Ms. Colman moved me up front where I could see better.)

After I checked off my best friends, I checked off my best enemy. Her name is Pamela Harding. She can be a meanie-mo sometimes. Her best friends are Jannie Gil-bert and Leslie Morris. I checked them off too.

Next I checked off Addie Sidney. She was arranging a collection of fall leaves on her wheelchair tray. She looked up at me and smiled.

Then Natalie Springer popped up from under her desk and banged her head. Poor Natalie. She had probably been pulling up her socks. They are always drooping. I checked off her name.

I checked off Ricky Torres, my pretend husband. (We got married on the playground one day at recess.) I checked off Bobby

Gianelli, Hank Reubens, and Omar Harris.

Terri and Tammy Barkan, who are twins, were in class. So was Audrey Green. Check. Check. Check.

I checked off a few more names. Then I handed the book and pencil back to Ms. Colman.

"Thank you, Karen," she replied. "All right, class. It is October. What holiday is coming up at the end of the month?"

"Halloween!" I shouted.

Oops. I know I am not supposed to shout or call out. At least this time I was not the only one. A few of us forgot the rules. That is because we were all excited about Halloween.

"It would be nice to do something together to celebrate the holiday," said Ms. Colman. "As usual, we will have our school costume parade. And our class can always have a party. But I thought we could think of something even more special. Does anyone have any ideas?"

Hoot! Hoot! Our class pet is a guinea pig. Sometimes he whistles and hoots in his cage.

"Maybe Hootie has an idea!" said Hannie.

Everyone laughed. But Hootie's hoot gave *me* an idea. It was a gigundoly good one too. I raised my hand, and Ms. Colman called on me.

"I think we should have a Halloween *pet* party," I said. "We can each bring a pet to school. We can dress our pets up in costumes!"

"That sounds like fun," said Ms. Colman. "But what about the children who do not have pets?"

"We can share," said Hannie.

"Good idea," said Ms. Colman.

"We can make paper pets too," I said. "Those pets will be very well behaved."

That made everyone laugh.

Hoot! Hoot!

"We will need a costume for Hootie," said Ricky.

I was proud of my husband for having such a good idea.

"We should have Halloween treats for everyone — people and pets," said Addie. "Candy for kids. Biscuits for dogs. Seed for birds."

Everyone was filled with ideas. We had lots of fun planning our party. Ms. Colman said we would hold the party after recess, before the school Halloween parade. I could not wait.

Who's a Party Pet?

Daddy was in his office when I returned from school. Sometimes he closes the door. That means he is busy working and should not be interrupted unless it is important. But his door was open. So I ran in to tell him about my day.

"Guess what! We are having a Halloween party at school. It is going to be a *pet party*. We can dress our pets in costumes. And it was my idea!" I said.

"That is terrific," replied Daddy. "Who are you planning to bring?"

23

"Well, I cannot bring the pet in myself. Ms. Colman says a grown-up has to bring our pets to school and take them home after the party," I said.

"That will not be a problem," said Daddy. "Elizabeth, Nannie, or I can come to school."

"Thank you," I said. "Now all I have to do is figure out which pet should come to the party. I was thinking about Scout. She is so cute and lively. But there are lots of special rules for guide-dogs-in-training. It might be hard to follow them at a party."

"I agree," said Daddy.

"Then I thought of Shannon. But she is too big and wild."

"I agree again."

"I do not want to bring Crystal Light or Goldfishie. They would just slosh around in their bowls. It would be more fun to bring Emily Junior. But one of the boys in our class is afraid of rats," I said.

"It is considerate of you to think of that," said Daddy.

24

(I was glad Daddy noticed how thought-ful I was being.)

"Of course, our new kitten would be per-fect," I said. "But we might not have the kit-ten in time for the party."

"Agreed," said Daddy.

"So that leaves Boo-Boo," I said.

Before I had a chance to say anything else, Daddy said, "Oh, no, Karen. You cannot bring Boo-Boo."

"Why not? Ever since we went to see Dr. Smith, Boo-Boo has been calmer. He did not even hiss at the other animals in the waiting room."

"If he seems calmer, it is because he is old and slowing down," said Daddy. "The party would be too much for him."

"But we are going to dress up our pets for Halloween. Boo-Boo would look cute in a costume," I said.

"He would not like being dressed up. You know that," said Daddy.

"I will make it fun for him. I promise. I will bring special treats for old cats. I will

25

put a cozy blanket in his carrier. I will not let anyone touch him. I will watch him every second."

"Karen, the answer is no. Absolutely not," said Daddy. "Boo-Boo is too old to go to school with you, especially for a party."

I had one thing to say. But I did not say it out loud. I said it to myself. Boo.

Big Plans

I have more pets than anyone I know, but not one of them was the right one to bring to school. I did not say another word about Boo-Boo and the party.

That night at dinner, we were eating our dessert when Sam said, "I left a copy of the *Stoneybrook Express* in the den. I did not have a chance to look at the pet ads. Has anyone else read them?"

"I have not. But I will do it right now!" I said.

"If you bring the paper in, we can read

the ads together," said Daddy.

I ran for the paper and handed it to Daddy. I was too excited to look for the ad page. Daddy found it toward the back of the paper. He started reading the ads out loud.

"I see several ads for puppies," said Daddy. "There are German shepherds, Yorkshire terriers, and poodles."

"Really?" I said.

All of a sudden I wanted another puppy. Puppies are very cute.

"Do not get any ideas, Karen. We are already a two-puppy house," said Nannie.

"And we voted to get a kitten, remember?" said Charlie.

"Oh, right," I replied.

Daddy was still reading the paper.

"There is an ad for a lost dog named Woof," he said. "He is a black cocker spaniel."

"That is so sad," said Kristy.

"I see an ad for parakeets. And one for a snake," said Daddy.

"Ooh, snakes are cool," said David Michael.

"We voted for a kitten," said Charlie.

"I see an ad for an older cat," said Daddy. "But there are no ads for kittens today."

"In a way that is good news," said Elizabeth. "There are usually too many kittens and not enough homes for them."

"Turn the page, please, Daddy," I said. "Maybe there are more ads on the next page. Maybe there is a special kitten page and we just missed it."

Daddy turned the page.

"There are only car ads here," he said.

"The paper comes out again on Friday," said Sam. "We can look then."

"Friday? I cannot wait till Friday! I want our kitten *now*!" I said. "I have big plans. I want to make a little bed for the kitten in my room. I want to teach the kitten to walk on a leash. I want to make a special food dish with the kitten's name on it!"

"Whoa!" said Charlie. "Maybe you should leave a few things for the rest of us to do."

"There is still a lot," I replied.

I decided it was not a good time to tell everyone the great name I had picked for the kitten. Even though I knew they would love it.

Everything was ready. All I needed was the kitten.

A Little Talk

Knock, knock. It was Kristy.

"Um, Karen, may I talk to you for a minute?" she asked.

I was in my room getting ready for bed.

"Sure," I replied. "What do you want to talk about?"

"I was listening to all the plans you have made for the kitten. They are very good ones," said Kristy. "But I want to make sure you heard what Charlie said. You need to leave things for the rest of us to do. The kitten will not belong only to *you*. The kitten will belong to the whole family."

"I know that," I said. "But someone has to take special care of it."

"We will all want to take care of the kitten," said Kristy. "It will make us feel better now, during the sad time."

"What sad time?" I asked.

"Don't you know, Karen? You went to the vet with my mom and Boo-Boo. You should know how sick he is," said Kristy.

"He is old," I replied. "It is not that sad. He is just a little slower than he used to be. He was never much fun to play with anyway."

"Well, I am sad even if you are not," said Kristy. "You should take some time to think about Boo-Boo. And please remember that any kitten who comes to live here will belong to all of us. You cannot be too bossy about taking care of him."

"I promise I will not be bossy," I said.

"And will you remember to think about Boo-Boo?" asked Kristy.

"I will remember."

"Good night," said Kristy.

"Good night," I replied.

As soon as Kristy left, I thought about my plans for the kitten again. I thought about putting the kitten bed on the floor. But maybe the kitten would be happier on my pillow. That would be so cozy. I would have three cats to sleep with. Goosie and Moosie, who are my stuffed cats, and Pumpkin.

Pumpkin. That is the name I picked. I was very happy with it. It was a good name for a boy kitten or a girl kitten. And it would be just right for a kitten who came to live with us around Halloween.

Of course, the kitten would be an orange tiger-striped one. It would have to be, with a name like Pumpkin. I just loved saying that name.

I was saying it to myself when I saw Boo-Boo pass by my room. I stopped and thought a minute about Boo-Boo, just like I had promised. At least I tried. But what was there to think about? Boo-Boo already had a name. He did not need a new bed or a new dish. I could not teach him any tricks. He was too old to learn them. And anyway, he was too cranky.

There. That did it. I had thought about Boo-Boo. Now I could think about Pumpkin — my little orange tiger-striped kitten.

Boo! Boo!

"**D**id you decide which pet you are going to bring to the party, Hannie?" I asked.

I was with Hannie and Nancy on the swings at recess.

Hannie has three pets. They are Myrtle the Turtle, Noodle the Poodle, and Pat the Cat.

"I wanted to bring all three," said Hannie. "I thought it would be fun to have them at school together. And then I would have extra pets to share with kids who do not have any."

"That is a good idea," said Nancy.

"I know. But my mother said she will only bring Myrtle the turtle. That is because Myrtle is small and easy to travel with."

"Myrtle will be a good pet to have at school," I said. "What about you, Nancy? Will your mom or dad bring Pokey?"

Pokey is one of the kittens who was born in the toolshed. Nancy got to keep him.

"Yes, Daddy will bring Pokey in," Nancy said. "How about you? You have so many pets. Which one is coming?"

"I have not decided yet," I replied. "All I know is that my pet and I will have matching costumes."

"Cool idea!" said Hannie. "What are you going to be?"

Brrring!

Recess was over. I was glad. I had a lot of decisions to make. What pet to bring. What costume to wear.

Back inside the classroom, we went over our spelling words. (I am a very good speller and wrote every one right.)

Then Ms. Colman said, "This afternoon I

would like to make a list of the names and kinds of pets that will be coming to the party. Then I can make name tags and buy treats for them. We will go around the room, starting at the back. Hannie?"

"My mother is bringing Myrtle, my turtle," said Hannie.

"Great," said Ms. Colman. "Nancy?"

Nancy announced that Pokey was coming. Jannie said her cat, Eloise, would be at the party. Bobby, Hank, and Omar would be bringing their dogs. Chris would bring a rabbit. Terri and Tammy would bring a frog.

"Karen? Will one of your pets be at the party?" asked Ms. Colman.

"Sure!" I said.

Ms. Colman waited for me to say more. When I did not, she asked, "Will you tell me which pet it will be?"

"Sure!" I replied.

Ms. Colman waited some more. While she was waiting, I was thinking. I had to say something fast. I could not keep her waiting any longer.

"Boo-Boo," I said at last.

A few kids laughed.

"I do not mean a boo-boo like you are hurt. I mean 'Boo! Boo!' like ghosts say."

"You could not have asked for a better Halloween name," said Ms. Colman. "What kind of pet is Boo-Boo?"

"A cat," I replied.

My turn was over and I was glad. My feelings were all mixed-up. I was happy I had a pet with a great Halloween name. But I was worried because my pet with the great Halloween name happened to be a pet I was not allowed to bring to the party.

"Psst, Karen? You are so lucky to be able to bring your cat," said Natalie. "My parents will not be able to bring in my mouse. So can I be your pet partner?"

Without thinking, I said, "Sure!"

Hmm. Bringing Boo-Boo was starting to sound like a great idea after all. He would have fun and Natalie would be happy. Maybe Daddy would change his mind.

Kittens!

When I went downstairs for breakfast on Friday morning, Sam and Charlie had their noses buried in the *Stoneybrook Express*.

"Is our kitten in there?" I asked.

Sam shook the paper. "Nope. No kittens here."

Sam likes to make jokes.

"Is there an ad for kittens?" I asked.

Just then Daddy entered the kitchen.

"We will look at the paper together after dinner tonight. If we start looking now, we will be late for work or school," he said.

"But what if there are kittens and someone calls before we do?" I asked.

"Then it was not meant to be," said Daddy. "What is meant to be now is for you to eat breakfast and get to school."

Oh, well. I did not need the kitten for the party. I was bringing Boo-Boo. I ate my Krispy Krunchies and went to the school bus stop.

All day I thought about the kitten who was going to be Pumpkin. I wondered what he was doing. Was he eating lunch when I was? Was he playing with his brothers and sisters while I was on the playground with Hannie and Nancy?

I daydreamed most of the afternoon. When I got home, I looked for the *Stoneybrook Express* but could not find it. Finally it was dinnertime. I ate as fast as I could.

"Should I get the paper now?" I asked, swallowing my last bite of spaghetti.

"I will get it as soon as everyone has finished eating," replied Daddy.

A couple of minutes later Daddy got the

paper. Sam and Charlie had circled two ads for litters of kittens.

Elizabeth called the first number, but all the kittens had been adopted already.

"I knew we should have called first thing in the morning!" I said.

Elizabeth called the second number. When she finished, she gave us the thumbs-up sign.

"The woman who placed the ad is Mrs. Cooper. She just got home from work and our call was the first one she answered," she said when she hung up the phone. "We can go see the kittens in the morning."

I could hardly wait! I counted kittens to fall asleep.

I saw kittens in my dreams at night. I saw them in my cereal bowl in the morning.

At nine o'clock on Saturday, we drove to Mrs. Cooper's house to see the litter.

"Look how cute they are!" I said.

Six kittens were playing in a box. Four were gray. One was black. And one was the orange tiger-striped kitten I had been hoping for!

"We will call you Pumpkin!" I said as if I had just thought of it.

I picked up the striped kitten and held him to my cheek. His paws were tiny and his eyes were big.

"Look, he is the cutest of all," I said.

But no one was looking at Pumpkin. Everyone was in a circle around Kristy. She was holding another one of the kittens. It was the black one.

"She is friendly and playful," I heard Daddy say.

The next thing I knew, Daddy was taking a vote.

"Whoever votes for the black kitten, say 'Aye,' " he said.

There were seven "ayes" and one "me."

"We will take this black kitten," said Daddy.

"She is twelve weeks old and will have all her shots and health tests by next week," said Mrs. Cooper. "If you come back next

Saturday, you can take your kitten home."

Before we left, I kissed Pumpkin on his warm head and put him gently back in the box. I was so disappointed.

Splat. A tear fell on his tiger-striped head.

Daddy's Cat

On the way home, everyone was talking about how great the black kitten was.

"We need to think of a name for her," said Kristy.

"We have a whole week to think of a name," said Elizabeth.

I tried not to let anyone see how unhappy I was. I did not want to seem like a baby. Daddy had taken a vote and the black kitten had won. I remembered what Kristy had said. The kitten was going to belong to the whole family, not just to me.

"Are you all right, Karen? You are awfully quiet," said Daddy on the way home.

"I am fine," I replied. "The black kitten is just not the one I liked best."

"I am sorry," said Daddy. "But she is an awfully nice kitten. I think you will grow to like her."

I did not think so, but I kept quiet. Had everyone forgotten that black cats are bad luck? And I guessed we would not be naming the kitten Pumpkin. How could a black cat be called Pumpkin?

When we got home, I sat in the den. I saw the *Stoneybrook Express* lying on a table and picked it up. Maybe there was another ad for kittens that we had not seen before. Maybe the black kitten would not pass her health tests. Maybe we would answer the other ad and there would be one tiger-striped kitten left. Just for us.

Maybe not. We were going to pick up the kitten next Saturday. She would probably be crabby like Boo-Boo. She would keep to herself and not want to play or be petted.

Meow!

Boo-Boo jumped up and sat on my lap. I was surprised. Boo-Boo did not usually do this. I wanted to pet him but I did not. I did not want him to run away.

Daddy sat down next to us. He petted Boo-Boo. Boo-Boo stayed. He even purred.

"So, Boo-Boo," said Daddy. "How do you think you will like having a new kitten in the family?"

Boo-Boo flicked his tail.

"Remember, the new kitten is not taking your place. No other cat can do that. You know we love you and we always will," said Daddy.

"You had Boo-Boo even before you had me," I said. "You had him even before you met Mommy, right?" I asked.

"Yes," said Daddy. "I brought Boo-Boo home from the shelter when I lived by myself. We kept each other company."

"Then it is sad that he is getting old," I said.

"Very sad. Boo-Boo and I are old friends. It is hard to see an old friend feeling bad," Daddy replied.

I petted Boo-Boo very lightly. He flicked his tail and purred. Poor old Boo-Boo. Maybe he was not such a bad cat after all.

There was a phone call for Daddy. When he stood up to answer it, Boo-Boo left too.

I sat and thought for awhile. I was sorry I had said some bad things about Boo-Boo lately. I was sorry for getting so excited about the new kitten and forgetting how Boo-Boo might be feeling. I was sorry for being disloyal to Daddy's old friend. I felt like a real meanie-mo.

But I was going to make things better with Boo-Boo and Daddy. Out of all my pets, I had picked Boo-Boo to go to my class party. That was very special. It was a good way to make up with Boo-Boo.

I knew Daddy did not think bringing

Boo-Boo to the party was a good idea. But he would change his mind. This was the best honor Boo-Boo could have. And the best way for me to show Daddy how much I loved his old friend.

The Bad-Luck Spell

Ouch! I had been out of bed for all of ten seconds on Sunday morning when I stubbed my toe. I sat down on the bed, rubbed my toe, and started over.

After breakfast the phone rang. It was Hannie.

"I know I said we could play today. But I have to go visit my aunt and uncle. I am sorry," she said.

"That is okay," I replied. "I will see you tomorrow."

Hmm. So far this was not my lucky day. I

knew something that would cheer me up. Talking to Mommy, Seth, and Andrew in Chicago. I asked Daddy if I could call them.

"Of course," he said. "This is a good time to call. It is early and they will probably be home."

They were home, but it was not a good time to call. That is because they had bad news for me.

"We all want to be with you so much, Karen. But Seth is going to have to work here in Chicago a little longer than we expected. We will not be back till late November. I promise we will be home for Thanksgiving," said Mommy.

"Thanksgiving! That is so far away. It is not even Halloween yet," I said.

"I am so sorry," said Mommy. "But we have no choice."

I talked to Mommy a little longer. Then I talked to Seth and Andrew. But the call did not cheer me up. When I hung up, I felt worse.

54

I looked outside. It was raining. I wondered if that was more bad luck. Then I decided it was a good thing. I would stay inside and do quiet things. But while I was drawing pictures, my purple marker ran out of ink. No one could drive me downtown to buy another, so I had to draw pictures without purple.

I was glad when Sunday was over. Monday started out a whole lot better. I reached school without anything bad happening. And in class something good happened. We had a spelling bee, and guess who won. If you guessed me, you are R-I-G-H-T!

Then my luck started to change again. I spilled my milk during lunch. And at recess, Hannie, Nancy, and I headed over to the swings. But Pamela, Jannie, and Leslie got to them just before we did.

"You had better be careful," I said to my friends. "My bad luck may be catching."

After school I went outside to meet Daddy. I usually ride home on the school bus, but Daddy had said he was going to be out with the car anyway and would drive Hannie and me home.

"Are you sure you want to come home in the car with me? Thanks to me, we might get a flat tire," I said to Hannie.

"I am not worried. Anyway, I already told my mom I would be going with you."

"Hi, Karen! Hi, Hannie!" called Daddy when he saw us. "How was your day?"

"It was okay," I said.

"Karen is having bad luck today. You had better check your tires," said Hannie.

Daddy laughed. "My tires are fine, thank you. Jump in and buckle up."

On the way home, Hannie and I talked about our Halloween costumes.

"I am thinking of dressing as a jack-o'-lantern," said Hannie. "And I might dress Myrtle up as a ghost. I will throw a white handkerchief over her shell."

"I am thinking of being a lion tamer. Boo-Boo will be the lion," I said. "Or maybe I will be Santa Claus and Boo-Boo can be one of my reindeer."

"Excuse me for interrupting," said Daddy. "But Karen, I must remind you that Boo-Boo is not going to your class party. We will talk more about this later."

Oops. I had not told Daddy about my latest party plan. If Hannie and I had been on the bus as usual, Daddy would not have heard me talking. More bad luck.

Suddenly I realized where all my bad luck was coming from. The black kitten. I knew my family should not have picked that cat. I knew it.

Down in the Dumps

When we returned home, Daddy and I went into his office to have our talk.

"I thought you would be happy," I said. "I thought it would be a great honor for Boo-Boo to be at the party."

"I am sure you meant well," said Daddy. "But I cannot change my mind about this. I see Boo-Boo growing more tired every day. He needs his routines. He needs peace and quiet. Taking him to the party is out of the question. I thought you understood that."

"I do understand — I guess. When I am

feeling sick or tired, I just want to stay home in my own bed. I would not want to go to a party either," I said.

"Thank you for thinking about this so carefully," said Daddy.

"You are welcome."

"I want to tell you a story about Boo-Boo I do not think I have told you before," Daddy went on.

"Okay," I replied.

"It is about the day I got Boo-Boo at the animal shelter. He had been brought in with five other kittens from a farmhouse. The family had all the cats they could handle and wanted to find good homes for these kittens," said Daddy. "I looked for a long time at the kittens. They were four months old and each one was cuter than the next. Finally I decided on the black kitten. I picked her up, and you know what happened? The gray tiger-striped kitten came along and mewed. He stood up on his hind legs and batted his paws in the air."

"Boo-Boo?" I said.

"He was not Boo-Boo yet, but he was going to be," said Daddy. "The man working at the shelter said he had never seen the gray kitten act that way before. 'He must be trying to tell you something,' the man said. When I put the black kitten down, she ran off to play with her brothers and sisters. But the gray kitten stayed behind. I picked him up. As soon as I did, he snuggled in my arms and went to sleep."

"So you did not pick Boo-Boo. Boo-Boo picked you," I said.

"That is right. I named him Boo-Boo to remind me that I almost made a boo-boo by leaving him behind," said Daddy. "Now, how about an afternoon snack? I do not know about you, but I am hungry."

"Me too," I replied.

"If you go wash up, I will have something good waiting when you get back," said Daddy.

I ran upstairs to wash. And to think. I knew Daddy's decision about Boo-Boo and the party was final. I guess it had been final before, but I had not wanted to listen. I had wanted to have my own way. Bringing Boo-Boo to the party would have been more of a good thing for me than for Boo-Boo or Daddy.

How could I show Daddy I was sorry? Maybe by not paying any attention to the kitten when we got it. Daddy would see that I did not love the kitten more than I loved Boo-Boo. That would make Boo-Boo happy. And Kristy, too, because I would not be acting bossy. That would make everyone happy. Except me.

I did not have time to think about all these things. I still had to think about the party. Now I had to start all over again, thinking about what pet to bring.

I was down in the dumps. But that did not stop me from being hungry. I finished washing and went downstairs for my snack.

Karen and Boo-Boo

At dinnertime on Friday, Mrs. Cooper called and spoke to Elizabeth.

"Your kitten has had all her shots and tests. She is frisky, healthy, and ready for her new home," Mrs. Cooper said.

I should have been happy. And I was, mostly. But I was worried too. I was worried that the kitten would not be as nice as everyone thought she was. And if she was nice and I liked her, I worried that I would hurt Daddy's feelings. Or Boo-Boo's. I worried that Boo-Boo might think the kitten was taking his place and we did not love him anymore.

I had enough worries to last all night and right into Saturday morning, when we drove to Mrs. Cooper's house.

Mrs. Cooper put our kitten into a travel box with a towel and a toy, and we brought her home.

"Here, kitty, kitty!" said Emily. "Meow!"

"It is so exciting to have a new kitten!" said Kristy.

Kristy had been worried that I would not share the new kitten with the family. But I hardly went near her. I stood back and watched. Boo-Boo was watching too.

"It is just you and me, Boo-Boo," I said.

There was one big difference. Boo-Boo did more than just watch. He hissed at the kitten. The kitten ignored him. I felt sorry for Boo-Boo. I could see he was not happy.

"Do not worry, Boo-Boo," I said. "Everyone still loves you. And remember, you are

the one I wanted to come to the Halloween party with me, not the kitten. Are you honored?"

Hsssss!

Boo-Boo was too busy hissing to be honored. Finally he got tired of hissing and went off to hide.

I stayed and watched the kitten for awhile. I had to admit she was cute. She had a shiny black coat and big green eyes. And she was very busy doing things.

First she batted a ball with a bell in it. *Ding! Ding!* Then she stopped playing with the ball and had a drink of water. We had put a little bowl next to Shannon's and Scout's big bowls. (Shannon and Scout were outside. We did not want them around when we brought the kitten home because they might scare her.) The kitten drank from one of the big bowls instead of her little one. She looked very funny. We all stayed close so we could scoop her out if she fell in.

Everyone in my family took turns picking

the kitten up and cuddling her. Even Daddy took a turn holding her.

"Have you held her yet, Karen?" asked Daddy.

"No. Maybe later I will. Right now I want to find Boo-Boo," I said.

"That is very thoughtful," said Daddy. "But I just checked on him and he is all right. He is hiding under my bed."

Poor Boo-Boo. I felt like hiding with him.

Pumpkin

I did not hide under the bed with Boo-Boo. I hid in my room until Nannie called me for lunch.

We were having our Saturday special. That is when we take the week's leftovers out of the refrigerator and spread them on the table. It is almost always my favorite meal of the week. But I did not feel much like eating. I could not get Boo-Boo to come near me. And I did not want to be around the new kitten.

In the kitchen everyone was busy filling their plates. But things seemed awfully quiet.

"Where is the kitten?" I asked.

"As soon as we brought out the tuna salad, she jumped up on the table," said David Michael.

"So we put her into her box for a nap," said Kristy. "She is just like a little baby in her crib."

"Where were you just before?" asked Charlie. "You missed the action. Before the kitten jumped onto the table, she did a somersault off the couch."

"Kitty fall down," said Emily.

"I think this kitten belongs in the circus!" said Sam.

Everyone was having so much fun. I felt left out.

After lunch, Daddy called for a family meeting to name the kitten. We sat together in the den to make suggestions and take a vote.

"Maybe we should call her Barnum, or Bailey, since she is such a good acrobat," said Sam.

"Kitty," said Emily.

"How about Midnight?" said David Michael. "Because she is so black."

"These are all good names," said Daddy. "Karen? Do you have any ideas?"

I usually have an idea a minute. But all I could think of just then was poor Boo-Boo, alone under the bed.

"Maybe we should call her Boo-Boo Too, in honor of Boo-Boo," I said.

"Is that t-o-o, which means *also*? Or t-w-o, which is the number?" asked Charlie.

"I was thinking of t-o-o because it is spelled like Boo-Boo," I said.

"We have so many good names to choose from now. Should we take our vote?" asked Nannie.

Everyone agreed it was time. But no one could agree on a name.

"I think Daddy should choose the name.

Whoever agrees with that, say 'Aye,' " I said.

The ayes won.

"Thank you for this honor," said Daddy. "Now, let me think."

He thought for a minute, then smiled.

"Karen, I heard you say the name Pumpkin when we went to Mrs. Cooper's house last week. I know our kitten is black, not orange. But she is joining our family just in time for Halloween. And I cannot get the name out of my head. So Pumpkin is my choice."

"Welcome to the family, Pumpkin!" said Charlie.

He lifted her out of her box. I was so happy!

Later, when Daddy was alone in the den, I said, "Thank you for picking the name Pumpkin. I like it even better than Boo-Boo Too."

"I thought so. But I appreciate your thinking of Boo-Boo," said Daddy. "I know he is not your favorite pet, and that is all right.

You are being respectful of him, and that is what counts."

I felt as though a big fat cat had been lifted from my shoulders. Daddy was not mad at me. I had been nice to Boo-Boo. And the name Daddy picked was Pumpkin. I felt like part of the family again.

Karen's Problem

When I got off the school bus on Monday morning, Natalie ran to me.

"Hi, Karen," she said. "Am I still your pet partner? How is Boo-Boo? Have you thought of a costume? Do you need any help? The party is on Friday, you know."

Uh-oh. I had forgotten all about the promise I made to Natalie.

"Yes, I know," I replied. "But I am afraid Boo-Boo is having a little problem. You see, he is getting very old. He is too old to come to school."

"You mean he got old in one week?" asked Natalie.

"No, he was old already. But he got more tired."

"Does that mean I cannot be your pet partner?" asked Natalie.

She looked very disappointed. Her lip started to quiver as if she were going to cry.

"You can be my partner. I just have to decide which pet to bring," I replied. "I will let you know very soon, okay?"

"Okay," said Natalie. "Just let me know before Friday. Mommy said I could buy the pet some special treats."

Natalie would be very happy if I brought in Pumpkin. Natalie had wanted one of Growly's kittens. She even took one home. But her parents said she was not allowed to have a kitten and made her bring it back.

Everyone in my class would love Pumpkin. But what if she brought bad luck? That would be terrible. And everyone would blame me for bringing her.

If I told my family I wanted to bring her

to school, they might say I was acting like she was my cat and nobody else's.

And what about Boo-Boo? It might not be respectful to bring Pumpkin to school after I had promised Boo-Boo he could come to the party. Daddy had said it was important to be respectful.

I was starting to wish I could be somebody's pet partner.

That gave me an idea. At lunchtime I talked to my friends.

"I cannot decide on which pet to bring to school for the party," I said.

"I thought you were bringing Boo-Boo," said Nancy.

I told them about my talk with Daddy.

"So I was wondering, Hannie, could I bring Pat the Cat? That would solve my problem," I said.

"Sure. But I think it would be more fun for everyone to meet Pumpkin. She is such a sweet kitten," said Hannie. (Hannie and Pumpkin had met the night before.)

I sighed.

"You are right," I said. "I will think about it some more and let you know if I need Pat the Cat."

I could not decide what to do. I was glad Mr. Mackey, our art teacher, was coming to our class later. Maybe I would make a paper pet. That would solve everything.

A Two-Cat Family

*M*ew!

I was up in my room doing my home-work. I turned and saw Pumpkin in my doorway. She looked so little there.

"Hello, Pumpkin," I said. "What are you up to?"

Mew!

She leaped into my room. Then she started to go wild. I had crumpled up a piece of paper and thrown it on the floor. Pumpkin pounced on it. She jumped off, then came back and hit it with her paw. The

paper rolled under my dresser. That did not stop Pumpkin. She went after it.

When she came out again, she did not have the crumpled paper anymore. She came out with a pair of rolled-up striped socks. (I had been looking for them all weekend.)

Swat! Swat-swat! She batted the socks back and forth between her paws.

I saw a shadow pass by my doorway. It was a Boo-Boo–sized shadow. He must have seen Pumpkin come into my room. Maybe he was jealous and hurt. Maybe he thought that I had invited Pumpkin in and not him.

I ran out to comfort him. But as soon as he saw me, he ran away.

"Poor Boo-Boo. I only wanted to pet you," I said.

For a moment I was angry with Pumpkin for making Boo-Boo feel bad. But it was not Pumpkin's fault. She was just a kitten who had come to play. She did not mean to hurt Boo-Boo's feelings. I went back into my room.

But Pumpkin was finished playing. She darted past me as fast as she had come in. *Mew!* I guess that was Pumpkin's way of saying good-bye.

Pumpkin turned up again later. I was in bed reading before going to sleep. (I had borrowed *Churchkitten Stories* from the school library.)

"Welcome back, Pumpkin," I said.

She jumped onto my bed and curled up next to me. She had a sweet smell and was soft and warm. I petted her and she started to purr.

Boo-Boo hardly ever lets me pet him. He keeps to himself most of the time. I looked toward the doorway but did not see any shadows.

"Boo-Boo, if you are there, you are going to have to try to understand. We are a two-cat family now. I can love two cats at once, Boo-Boo. Just the way I love Goosie and Moosie. Just the way Mommy and Daddy love Andrew and me," I said.

Then I thought of something else.

"Hey, Boo-Boo, if you are there, I have something for you to think about. Please think about being friends with Pumpkin," I said.

I looked at Pumpkin. She was such a friendly kitten. I was sure she would be friends with Boo-Boo if he would let her.

"Please try, Boo-Boo, please," I said.

Pumpkin snuggled closer to me and closed her eyes. Out of everyone in my family, she had picked me to sleep with.

"Pumpkin, I love you!" I whispered.

Pumpkin opened her eyes and looked at me.

Mew! I guess that was Pumpkin's way of saying I love you back.

Decision Day

When I woke up on Tuesday morning, Pumpkin was not in my bed. She had probably gone downstairs for her breakfast.

I washed, got dressed, and headed downstairs too.

It was decision day. I had to decide which pet I was going to bring to the party and what costumes we would wear.

Ms. Colman needed to know so she could make up the right name tag.

I had promised Natalie I would tell her so she and her mom could buy treats.

I needed to know myself, so I could stop worrying and start looking forward to our party.

Luckily everyone was in the kitchen at once.

"Attention, please!" I said. "By now you all know that my class is having a Halloween pet party. I would like to invite Pumpkin to it. I know she is the family's pet, not just mine. But I would still like to bring her to school. I promise to take good care of her. Is that okay?"

Daddy took a vote, and everyone agreed Pumpkin could go to the party. Daddy said he would bring her himself.

"Thank you very much. Enjoy your breakfast," I said.

My announcement was over. And my decision was made.

I looked for Pumpkin so I could tell her the good news. I found her curled up in her box, snoozing. (Kittens need plenty of rest too.) I decided to tell her the news when I came home from school.

Then I looked for Boo-Boo. I wanted to make sure there were no hard feelings. I found him curled up under the hall table. But he was not snoozing. His eyes were open.

"Boo-Boo, you are not going to the party. But I think it is better that way. The truth is, you would not really like a crowded, noisy room full of kids. You do not like being petted much, and that is what everyone would try to do. So I hope you know that you are staying home for your own good and not because I do not want to bring you to school."

Boo-Boo flicked his tail. I think he understood.

On the bus ride to school, I told Hannie that Pumpkin was coming to the party.

"That will be so much fun!" she said. "What costumes are you going to wear?"

My last decision was an easy one. I did not even have to think. I picked my all-time favorite Halloween costume. I had the perfect pet to go with it.

"I am going to be a witch, and Pumpkin will be my black cat!" I said.

At school I told Ms. Colman that Pumpkin was coming instead of Boo-Boo. She said she would be happy to change the name tag.

Natalie was thrilled that she would get to meet Pumpkin. After school she was going to buy the best treats she could find.

And in art class I made a little black witch hat for Pumpkin to wear to the party.

There were three more days till party time. I could hardly wait.

The Halloween Party

When I woke up on Friday morning, I was glad to see the sun shining. I did not want Pumpkin to have to travel in the rain.

I dressed, ate, then packed up my witch's costume and Pumpkin's black hat. (I had brought the hat home to be sure it fit Pumpkin.)

"See you later, Daddy," I said. "See you later, Pumpkin!"

At school everyone was excited. Ms. Colman knew all we could think about was Halloween and our party. But we still had spelling and math work to do. So we had a Halloween spelling bee. Ms. Colman called it "Which Witch Is Which?" and gave us only words about Halloween to spell.

For math we counted the number of pets who would be at our party, and how many categories of pets there would be. (I told Ms. Colman that the word *cat*egories was an excellent word for our pet party.) We counted eleven live pets and six paper pets. And there were seven different kinds — dogs, cats, bird, frog, turtle, rabbit, and guinea pig.

After recess we rearranged the tables so the middle of the room would be open for our party. We put on our costumes. Then the grown-ups and pets started filing in.

Woof! Meow! Tweet! Hoot-hoot!

Our classroom was wild! Not everyone behaved well. Bobby's dog started growling at Hank's dog and they had to stand on opposite sides of the room.

Then Omar's big frisky dog knocked over two chairs on his way in.

Nancy's kitten, Pokey, threw up a hair ball. (Some kids were worried. But Nancy said Pokey had done it lots of times before.)

"Where is Pumpkin?" asked Natalie. "I cannot wait to meet her."

"I am sure she will be here soon," I said.

I was getting a little worried. Most of the animals had already arrived and were wearing their costumes.

What if Daddy had changed his mind about bringing Pumpkin in? What if Pumpkin had gotten sick? But I knew I did not really have to worry. Daddy would call if there were a problem.

Finally Daddy walked into the room with Pumpkin. I ran to greet them.

"Hello, Pumpkin, how was your trip?" I asked.

"I am sorry we are late," said Daddy. "I had trouble catching Pumpkin and putting her into her box."

"She was probably excited about the party," I replied. "Natalie, come meet Pumpkin!"

I introduced Natalie to Pumpkin.

"She is so sweet. You are really lucky," said Natalie.

She gave Pumpkin the fish-shaped treats she had brought. Pumpkin loved them. Then Nancy held out Pokey. We introduced Pumpkin and Pokey and they liked each other right away.

I was already wearing my witch's costume. It was time to put on Pumpkin's hat. I set it on her head, but it slid off. I put it back on. It slid off again. The third time it slid off, I left it hanging. Pumpkin started playing with it.

"Wait, Pumpkin. Do not ruin your costume yet," I said.

Ms. Colman was calling for our attention. She was holding a camera.

"Welcome, everyone," said Ms. Colman. "Please stand as close together as you can. I would like to get a picture of the guests at our Halloween pet party."

I put the hat back on Pumpkin's head. I

held Pumpkin in my arms. Natalie stood by me and held the hat in place.

"Ready?" said Ms. Colman. "Say 'Happy Halloween!' "

"Happy Halloween!" we called.

Click! Ms. Colman took our picture. Then she gave out treats and awards. Every pet got one. Pumpkin's award was for youngest pet at the party.

"You are very special, Pumpkin," I said.

Pumpkin was also very tired. She curled up on the desk between Natalie and me and fell fast asleep.

Cat Lessons

"This is how you do it," I said to Pumpkin.

It was Saturday morning. I was giving Pumpkin her first walking-on-a-leash lesson.

It had taken me a long time to find Pumpkin, because she was playing hide-and-seek with me. It took even longer to put on her leash, because she kept squirming away. Finally I snapped the leash on.

I was about to start her lesson when I saw Boo-Boo peeking out from behind the couch. Daddy had said he did not think

Boo-Boo would like walking on a leash. But I was not so sure. And I had an extra leash to try with.

I called for Daddy.

"I think Boo-Boo feels left out," I said. "I think he might want a leash too."

"We can try," Daddy replied.

Guess what. Boo-Boo let Daddy put the leash on.

"Will you stay and help me, Daddy?" I asked.

"Sure," Daddy replied. "I am already amazed. Boo-Boo seems to be perking up a little bit."

I tried to remember the hints about walking cats on leashes that I had heard on a radio show about pets. But none of them was working. Maybe I did not remember them well. Maybe I needed a book. Maybe I needed more cooperative cats.

Pumpkin was too young and frisky. She walked two steps with me, then stood up on her back paws and started batting at the leash with her front paws.

Boo-Boo was too old and short-tempered. He decided he did not like the leash after all. He lay down on the floor and started biting it.

"Oh, well," said Daddy. "We tried."

He took the leash off of Boo-Boo. I took the leash off of Pumpkin.

"I am going to help get lunch ready," Daddy said. "I will call you when it is time to eat."

I sat down on the floor next to Boo-Boo. The next thing I knew, Pumpkin had jumped onto my lap. Boo-Boo did not get up and run away.

I decided it was a good time to have a little talk with them both.

"So, Boo-Boo, how do you like having a new kitten in the house?" I asked.

Boo-Boo looked up at me and flicked his tail.

"I know you and Pumpkin are different in some ways. You are old. Pumpkin is young. You are gray with stripes. Pumpkin is black," I said. "But you have a lot in common too. You are both cats. Neither of you will let me walk you on a leash. And there is one more important thing. I love you both a lot."

I reached down and petted Boo-Boo with my left hand and Pumpkin with my right. And they purred softly together.

"I think the three of us are going to be okay," I said. I felt like purring too.

L. GODWIN

About the Author

ANN M. MARTIN lives in New York City and loves animals, especially cats. She has two cats of her own, Gussie and Woody.

Other books by Ann M. Martin that you might enjoy are *Stage Fright*; *Me and Katie (the Pest)*; and the books in *The Baby-sitters Club* series.

Ann likes ice cream and *I Love Lucy*. And she has her own little sister, whose name is Jane.

BABY·SITTERS
Little Sister

Don't miss #103

KAREN'S MOVIE STAR

She turned to look at me, then she smiled. "Hello. You're the Brewer girl, aren't you?"

"Yes," I said eagerly. "I'm Karen Brewer. These are my friends Hannie Papadakis and Nancy Dawes. We are here to audition for a part together. We are all best friends."

"Oh, good," said Ms. Wynoski.

"In fact," I continued quickly, "I have prepared a poem to recite. 'I think that I shall never see — ' "

"Just a moment, Karen," said Ms. Wynoski, holding up her hand. "These are non-speaking roles. Bill? Could you come here, please?"

I wanted to continue with my poem, but Ms. Wynoski was talking to one of the men who had been choosing kids. He looked at us and nodded, then walked away.

"Guess what?" said Ms. Wynoski. "I think you three best friends just got walk-on parts in the crowd scene."

Little Sister

by Ann M. Martin
author of The Baby-sitters Club®

More Titles... ➡

♥ ♥

The Baby-sitters Little Sister titles continued...

❏	MQ26301-3	#73	Karen's Dinosaur	$2.95
❏	MQ26214-9	#74	Karen's Softball Mystery	$2.95
❏	MQ69183-X	#75	Karen's County Fair	$2.95
❏	MQ69184-8	#76	Karen's Magic Garden	$2.95
❏	MQ69185-6	#77	Karen's School Surprise	$2.99
❏	MQ69186-4	#78	Karen's Half Birthday	$2.99
❏	MQ69187-2	#79	Karen's Big Fight	$2.99
❏	MQ69188-0	#80	Karen's Christmas Tree	$2.99
❏	MQ69189-9	#81	Karen's Accident	$2.99
❏	MQ69190-2	#82	Karen's Secret Valentine	$3.50
❏	MQ69191-0	#83	Karen's Bunny	$3.50
❏	MQ69192-9	#84	Karen's Big Job	$3.50
❏	MQ69193-7	#85	Karen's Treasure	$3.50
❏	MQ69194-5	#86	Karen's Telephone Trouble	$3.50
❏	MQ06585-8	#87	Karen's Pony Camp	$3.50
❏	MQ06586-6	#88	Karen's Puppet Show	$3.50
❏	MQ06587-4	#89	Karen's Unicorn	$3.50
❏	MQ06588-2	#90	Karen's Haunted House	$3.50
❏	MQ06589-0	#91	Karen's Pilgrim	$3.50
❏	MQ06590-4	#92	Karen's Sleigh Ride	$3.50
❏	MQ06591-2	#93	Karen's Cooking Contest	$3.50
❏	MQ06592-0	#94	Karen's Snow Princess	$3.50
❏	MQ06593-9	#95	Karen's Promise	$3.50
❏	MQ06594-7	#96	Karen's Big Move	$3.50
❏	MQ06595-5	#97	Karen's Paper Route	$3.50
❏	MQ06596-3	#98	Karen's Fishing Trip	$3.50
❏	MQ49760-X	#99	Karen's Big City Mystery	$3.50
❏	MQ50051-1	#100	Karen's Book	$3.50
❏	MQ50053-8	#101	Karen's Chain Letter	$3.50
❏	MQ50054-6	#102	Karen's Black Cat	$3.50
❏	MQ43647-3		Karen's Wish Super Special #1	$3.25
❏	MQ44834-X		Karen's Plane Trip Super Special #2	$3.25
❏	MQ44827-7		Karen's Mystery Super Special #3	$3.25
❏	MQ45644-X		Karen, Hannie, and Nancy The Three Musketeers Super Special #4	$2.95
❏	MQ45649-0		Karen's Baby Super Special #5	$3.50
❏	MQ46911-8		Karen's Campout Super Special #6	$3.25
❏	MQ55407-7		BSLS Jump Rope Pack	$5.99
❏	MQ73914-X		BSLS Playground Games Pack	$5.99
❏	MQ89735-7		BSLS Photo Scrapbook Book and Camera Pack	$9.99
❏	MQ47677-7		BSLS School Scrapbook	$2.95
❏	MQ13801-4		Baby-sitters Little Sister Laugh Pack	$6.99
❏	MQ26497-2		Karen's Summer Fill-In Book	$2.95

Available wherever you buy books, or use this order form.

Scholastic Inc., P.O. Box 7502, Jefferson City, MO 65102

Please send me the books I have checked above. I am enclosing $_____
(please add $2.00 to cover shipping and handling). Send check or money order – no cash or C.O.Ds please.

Name_____Birthdate_____

Address_____

City_____State/Zip_____

Please allow four to six weeks for delivery. Offer good in U.S.A. only. Sorry, mail orders are not available to residents of Canada. Prices subject to change.   BSLS398

♥ ♥